THE DAY OF A
COUNTRY VETERINARIAN

BY GAIL GIBBONS

Macmillan Publishing Company   New York   Maxwell Macmillan Canada   Toronto
Maxwell Macmillan International   New York   Oxford   Singapore   Sydney

To Wilton, Max,
Keats, Byron and Bramble

Also, in memory of
Milton

Special thanks to
Edwin Blaisdell, D.V.M., of North
Haverhill, New Hampshire. Also, special
thanks to Dr. Harold Brown, Dr. Barbara
Burroughs, and Dr. Cori Weiner of
Brown's Animal Hospital of
Burlington, Vermont.

10   9   8   7   6   5   4   3   2   1
Library of Congress Cataloging-in-Publication Data
Gibbons, Gail. Say woof! : the day of a country veterinarian / written and illustrated by Gail Gibbons. — 1st ed.   p.   cm. Summary: Describes the work of a veterinarian and some of the procedures and instruments he uses to treat animals in his office and on farms. Also tells how to take good care of pets. ISBN 0-02-736781-9   1. Veterinarians—Juvenile literature.   2. Veterinary medicine—Vocational guidance—Juvenile literature.   [1. Veterinary medicine.   2. Veterinarians.   3. Occupations.]   I. Title
SF756.G53   1992   636.089—dc20   91-48270

A dog, a kitten, a baby goat, a parakeet and another dog. They are all patients at the animal hospital. It is early morning, but people and their pets are already here.

They are waiting to see the veterinarian. A veterinarian is a doctor who takes care of animals, the way other doctors take care of people.

This country veterinarian loves animals and wants to help them. Before he could open his own animal hospital, he had to go to a special school after college, just as a doctor goes to medical school. He had to learn how to care for many different kinds of animals—pets and farm animals.

ASSISTANT

Before he sees his patients, the vet checks the animals that have stayed overnight. Some of them are boarders, staying at the animal hospital while their owners are away from home. Others are there because they are patients. The vet checks on a dog he operated on yesterday. All is well. Soon her owner will come to get her. An assistant has just finished cleaning their cages. She gives them fresh water and feeds the ones that need to be fed.

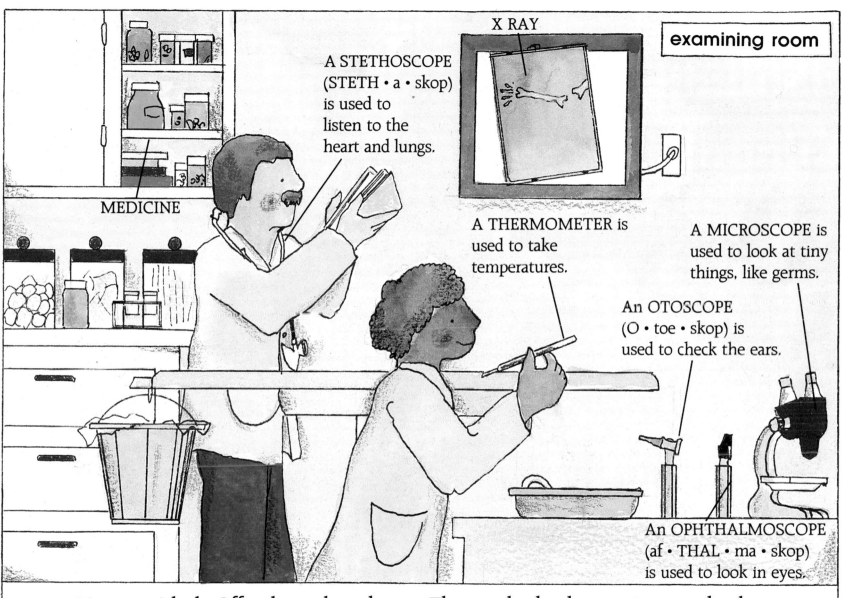

X RAY

A STETHOSCOPE (STETH • a • skop) is used to listen to the heart and lungs.

MEDICINE

A THERMOMETER is used to take temperatures.

A MICROSCOPE is used to look at tiny things, like germs.

An OTOSCOPE (O • toe • skop) is used to check the ears.

An OPHTHALMOSCOPE (af • THAL • ma • skop) is used to look in eyes.

It's nine o'clock. Office hours have begun. The vet checks the appointment book in his examining room. His other assistant makes sure all the medical tools are clean and ready.

Here's the first patient, a parakeet with a broken wing. The owner tells the vet that her bird flew into a wall. The vet gently feels where the break is and carefully puts a splint on it. "Come back in five days," he tells her. "I'll see how the wing is mending."

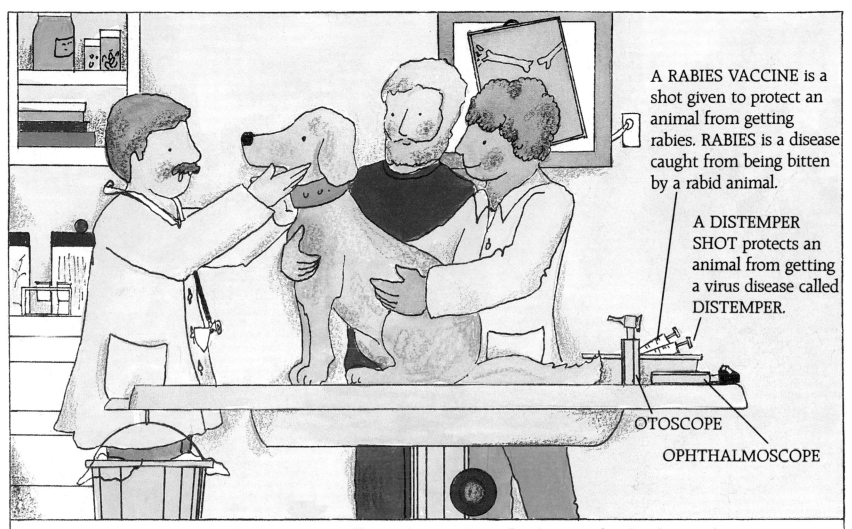

A RABIES VACCINE is a shot given to protect an animal from getting rabies. RABIES is a disease caught from being bitten by a rabid animal.

A DISTEMPER SHOT protects an animal from getting a virus disease called DISTEMPER.

OTOSCOPE

OPHTHALMOSCOPE

"Wilton is next," the assistant calls. Wilton is here for his yearly checkup. The vet examines his eyes and ears. He looks at the dog's fur. "Say woof!" the vet jokes as he looks down Wilton's throat. Next, the vet touches and feels his body and takes his temperature. Wilton is a healthy dog. All he needs to get is a rabies vaccine and distemper shot.

 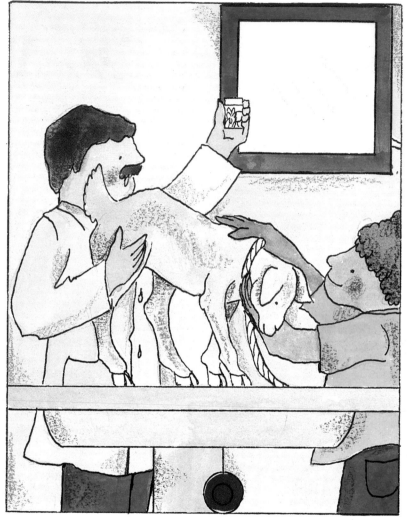

Who's next? A cute kitten! The vet examines him. He is in good health and only needs the few shots that all kittens are supposed to have. The next patient is a baby goat. She has a stomachache and won't eat. The vet looks her over and tells the owner she will be fine. "Just give her these pills three times a day," he says.

SET means to put back in its correct position.

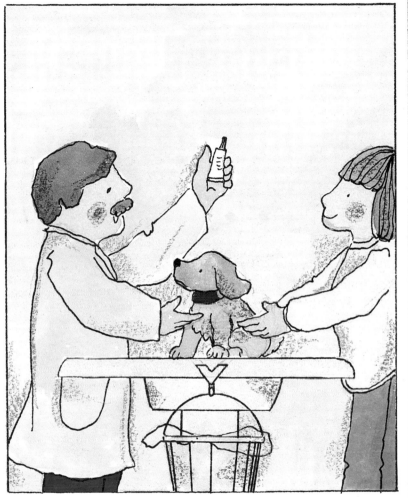

Emergency! Someone has just brought in a baby groundhog that was hit by a truck. It has a broken leg. The vet sets and splints the leg and tells his assistant to put the animal in one of the cages. Finally, he examines the dog that has been so patient out in the waiting room. She has an eye infection. "Put this ointment on her eye each day for a week. Then come back to see me," he tells the owner.

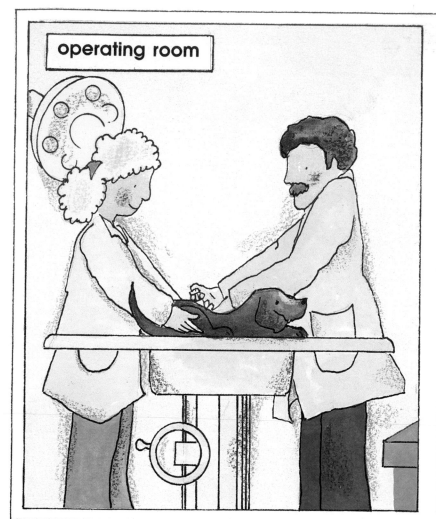

operating room

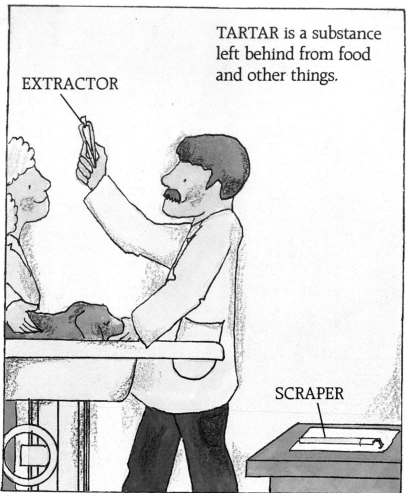

EXTRACTOR

TARTAR is a substance left behind from food and other things.

SCRAPER

It's eleven-o'clock. Surgery time. Two pets were boarded overnight because they are scheduled for surgery today. The first patient's name is Ben. Poor Ben has a toothache. The vet gives him a shot to put him to sleep. Then he finds Ben's bad tooth and pulls it out. While Ben is still asleep, the vet cleans the tartar from the rest of his teeth so they won't become infected.

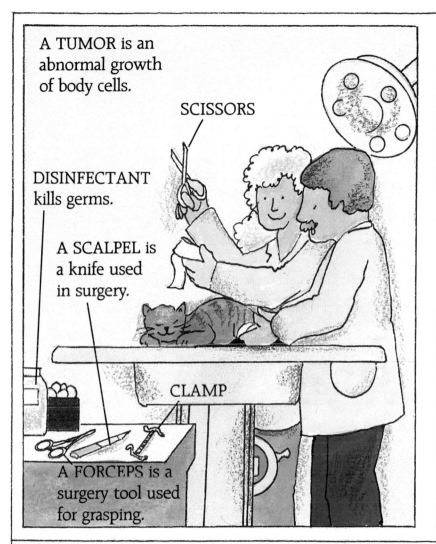

A TUMOR is an abnormal growth of body cells.

SCISSORS

DISINFECTANT kills germs.

A SCALPEL is a knife used in surgery.

CLAMP

A FORCEPS is a surgery tool used for grasping.

The other patient is a cat. She has a lump called a tumor on her leg. After her shot, she falls asleep. Slowly the vet cuts the tumor away and removes it. Then the cut is sutured, or stitched. The area is disinfected and bandaged with soft tape. They place her carefully back in her cage.

What a busy morning! Time to relax and have some lunch. The phone rings. It's another vet in a nearby town. She wants to know about a new medicine the vet has been using. Veterinarians must stay up to date on the latest medical improvements.

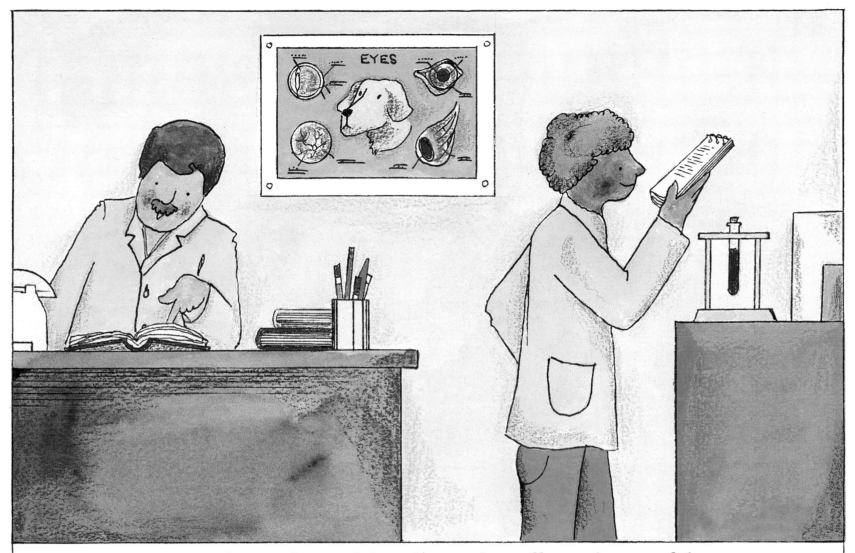

Country vets only spend part of their days in their offices. The rest of the time they are on the road taking care of animals on farms, at stables, and in homes. The vet checks his schedule book. Then he gathers up the blood samples he's taken from some of his patients to bring to a medical lab.

Outside, one of his assistants is at the truck, filling it with everything the vet might need to treat the animals they will see. Off they go.

BLOOD SAMPLE

BRUCELLOSIS (brew • sa • LOW • sis) is a disease that causes fever in cattle and people.

It's one-thirty. First stop. They arrive at a farm where the vet takes blood samples from the farmer's cows. This blood will be tested at a state lab to see if the cows have a disease called brucellosis. A farmer cannot sell milk or sell his cows for meat if they have this disease.

The next stop is a stable. One of the horses has a sore, lame leg. The vet gives her a shot to kill the pain. "I'll stop by tomorrow to see how she is doing," the vet says.

ANEMIC means there aren't enough red blood cells.

At the next stop a farmer has some new baby pigs. "Could you look them over?" the farmer asks. They squeal as the vet and his assistant check them. Each one gets an iron shot so they won't become anemic. They are very healthy piglets.

The next farm is a sheep farm. The vet cuts off, or docks, the lambs' tails. If he doesn't, their tails would get dirty and attract lots of flies that would bother them. It's best to do this when they are lambs because it doesn't hurt as much as it would when fully grown. The vet and his assistant hug each lamb. "Everything will be okay," they say.

A voice comes from the vet's truck. "Emergency!" Back at the office the assistant
is calling the vet over a special radio. "Yes?" he answers.
"Mrs. Miller's dog was just hit by a car. Please hurry over there!" the assistant says.
The vet and his assistant jump into the truck. Off they go!

Mrs. Miller is very upset. The vet gently feels her dog's body and legs to see if there are any broken bones. He listens with his stethoscope. All is well.

The vet looks into the dog's eyes. Then, he notes the color of its gums. They are nice and pink.

"He's more stunned than anything," the vet tells Mrs. Miller.

"He should be fine by tomorrow."

It's four-thirty. They stop at the lab to drop off the blood samples. The lab will have a report ready tomorrow. Then they head back to the office.

What a long day. It's six o'clock. The vet visits his two surgery patients in their cages. They're doing well and will be able to go home to their families tomorrow. He looks over his day book, the book he wrote in when he visited places today. He checks tomorrow's schedule, too.

One of the assistants jots down bills that have been paid. Cages are cleaned and the animals get fresh water. The little groundhog is doing fine. When he is older and all better, the vet plans to release him back into his natural home, the fields in the countryside.

It's time for the country veterinarian and his assistants to go home. Tonight might bring another emergency. If not, tomorrow will be another busy day of caring for animals.

CARING FOR YOUR PET

1. Your pet should have fresh water available all the time.

2. Feed your pet the right food regularly on schedule.

3. Some pets must be walked outside to go to the bathroom. Set aside time to do this. Other pets need a special place. Keep it clean.

LITTER BOX

BIRD FOOD

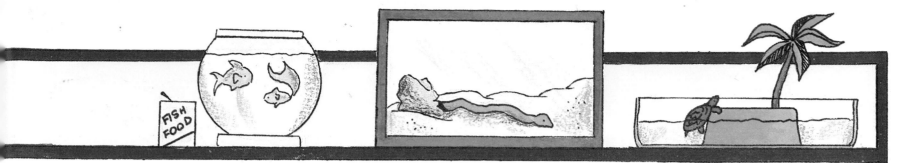

4. Some pets need special homes. Keep them clean.

5. Some pets need help keeping themselves clean, too.

6. Most pets need exercise to keep themselves healthy and happy.

7. Some pets play with toys. Make sure your pet has safe toys.

8. Many pets must go to the veterinarian for their yearly checkup. Make sure you do this.

9. If your pet looks sick or injured, bring it to your veterinarian.

Remember...
all pets need love and care just as you do.